Printed in USA

Published by: Leela Hope

© Copyright 2016

-

- **ISBN-10: 978-1532975622**

- **ISBN-13: 1532975627**

-

-

- **All Rights Reserved**
- No part of this publication may be reproduced
- or transmitted in any form whatsoever, electronic,
- or mechanical, including photocopying, recording,
- or by any informational storage or retrieval system
- without express written, dated and signed permission from the author.
-
- By reading this you accept these terms and conditions.

Wally Raccoon's Farmyard Olympics Athletics Day

By: Leela Hope

Wally Raccoon

Went for a walk.

When soon he saw

Henry the Hawk.

Henry was flying

And twirling about.

Excited, it seemed.

"For what? I'll find out!"

So Wally asked Henry

And Henry would say:

"The Farmyard Olympics

It's Athletics Day!"

Wally and Henry

Went down to the crowd,

Where Big Uncle Moe

Was standing quite proud.

"Our horses are winning

The hurdles this year.

There's no room for error

And no room for fear!"

"Can I race?" said Wally,

"In this hurdle course?"

"You can't jump these hurdles!"

Said the great big horse.

Then, everyone cheered

As the horses ran past.

But Wally was sad it looked like a blast!

So Wally moved on

In search of some fun.

His aim to compete perhaps in this one.

"Our dogs are all winning

In this discus toss.

Look Sal's in the lead."Said Old Rooster Gus.

"Can I play this sport?

I'll try it!"asked Wally.

But Gus simply laughed,

"Who's heard of such folly?"

Now Wally was sad

And feeling quite down,

When Scamp the Squirrel

Said,"What's with the frown?"

"They won't let me play,"

Wally said with a sob.

"Come with me,"said Scamp,

"And we'll ask Beaver Bob."

"But of course!" said Bob

With a grin on his face.

"A small creatures race and for you,there's a place!"

So Wally ran hard and as fast as he could.

No one could pass him there was no one who would!

Now Wally was glad that he got to compete

And there wasn't a team that his team couldn't beat.

Disclaimer - Legal Notes

Every effort has been made to accurately

represent this book and it's potential.

Results vary with every individual, and your results may or may not

be different from those depicted.

No promises, guarantees or warranties,

whether stated or implied, have been made that you

will produce any specific result from this book.

Your efforts are individual and unique,

and may vary from those shown.

Your success depends on your efforts, background and motivation.

The author shall in no event be held liable

for any loss or other damages caused by

the use and misuse of or inability to

use any or all of the information described in this book.

By using the information in this book,

you agree to do so entirely at your own risk.

Use of the programs, advice,

and information contained in this

book is at the sole choice and risk of the reader.

Some website links referred to in this book

may be affiliate links and as such the author

will earn a commission on any purchases made.

About the Author

Leela Hope is a writer with over 22 years of experience

in writing endearing children's fiction.

Her lively characters have entranced and

captivated her audience, and she has taken

great joy in writing the three series of books,

each beautifully illustrated with love and care.

Her stories concentrate on the adventures of floppy eared

bunnies and wide-eyed children learning lessons in life,

before returning home wiser and eager for sleep.

leela hope writes her stories to entertain the v

ery young, but also to educate.

Her vision is always of a parent sitting on a

child's bed, reciting

the stories each night,

while the young one drifts off to sleep,

lulled into a dream world full of fun and adventure.

From her very earliest years of childhood,

leela made up stories in her head, telling them to her younger brother and sister.

The stories flowed easily from her mind,

and it wasn't long before she realized she had

a gift for writing. By the age of 14, she had already written a small

book of short stories for her own entertainment,

and by the age of 22, she had published her first

full-fledged children's fiction in several magazines

leela hope was destined to be an author and she

knew exactly what genre of fiction she wanted to dedicate her life too.

Born in San Diego, California, and still residing in the area,

leela studied English Literature at Berkeley, earning a degree in 1989.

Her writing covers a span of several genres,

but she always returns to her first love,

children's fiction. She enjoys scuba diving and visiting wildlife parks,

seeking new inspiration for cuddly characters for her stories.

leela hope lives in an urban area of San Diego and is presently at work on a new book.

http://www.leelahope.net/

37687946R10015

Made in the USA
San Bernardino, CA
23 August 2016